Firenze's Light

By Jessica Collaço

Illustrated by Angela Li

SHINE YOUR LIGHT BOOKS

For my family - J.C.

Special Thanks to: Ann Bombich, Karyn Crispo, Tom and Lois Jaques, and The Lipinsky Family. This book was made possible by the generosity of Kickstarter backers. To each one of you, I am grateful.

Firenze's Light

www.shineyourlightbooks.com

Library of Congress Control Number: 2014901328
First Edition 10 9 8 7 6 5 4
ISBN: 978-0-9914607-0-0

Shine Your Light Books

Firenze likes dancing.

Firenze likes books.

But there is one thing Firenze does not like....

Firenze does not like her light.
"It's always shining at the WRONG TIME!"

At the movies.....

at slumber parties.....

during games of hide and seek.

"Your light makes you unique," said her Mother. "No one shines just like you."

"I'll cover up my light" Firenze thought. She gathered leaves and wrapped them around her until her light was hidden.

The next day Firenze's friends needed her help. At the movies, Tick dropped his snack under his seat. "Firenze, can you shine your light down here?"

"What light? I don't have a light!" snapped Firenze.

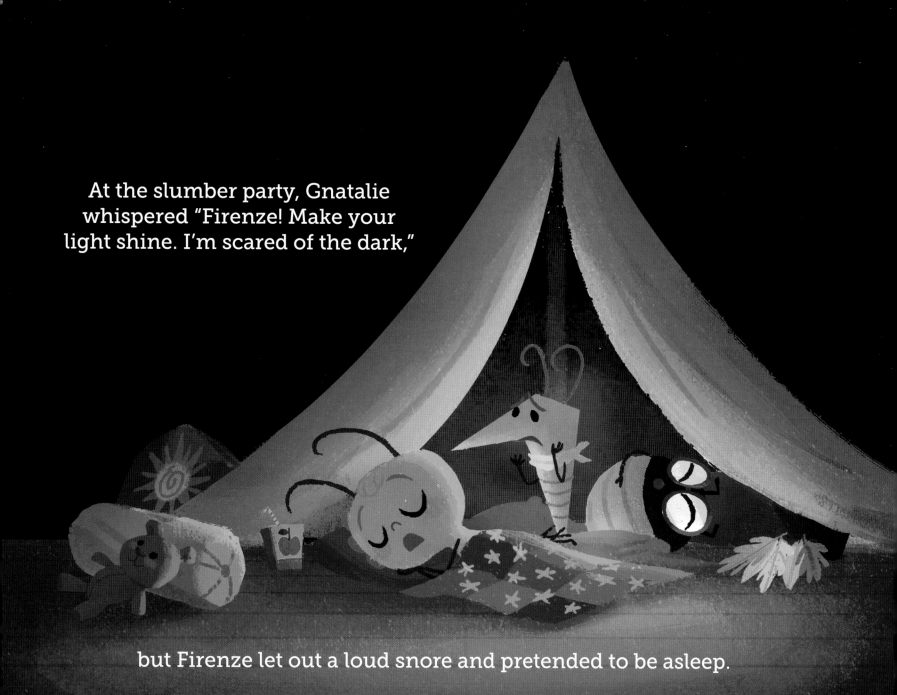

At the slumber party, Gnatalie whispered "Firenze! Make your light shine. I'm scared of the dark,"

but Firenze let out a loud snore and pretended to be asleep.

During a game of hide and seek, Firenze hid in her best spot, deep in the dark bushes.

"Come out, Firenze!" shouted Legs. "It's too hard to find you when your light doesn't shine"

"Come out, Firenze!"

but Firenze pretended not to hear and flew away as fast as she could.

Firenze found herself deep in the forest, far away from her friends.

She had hoped they would forget about her light. She felt very sad. Just as she began to cry, she heard a strange sound coming from the bushes behind her.

"Mmunch Mmunch Mmunch." Firenze flew closer to investigate.

Munch munch munch munch CRUNCH. I LOVE IT!

"What are you doing?" asked Firenze.

"Creating my MASTERPIECE!!!"exclaimed a beetle, clicking his huge pincers.

"I'm Kirie. I am using my magnificent pincers to make WONDERFUL ART!!! Isn't it AMAZING?!!"

"It's lovely," said Firenze.

As she looked at Kirie's art, Firenze's light began to **shine** through the patterns in the leaves.

"Oh how beautiful!" Firenze gasped, enchanted by the colors and shapes that appeared all around her.

"Wow!" whispered Kirie. "Your light is making my art even more magical. What a wonderful gift you have."

"Oh! No," said Firenze. "I don't like my light. I wish it would go away." She began grabbing leaves to wrap around herself.

"I understand," said Kirie. "I used to feel the same way about my pincers, but then I realized

I am BRILLIANT! I am WONDERFUL!
I am UNIQUE!!!"

"I wish I could feel like that about my light, Kirie, but I don't!" Firenze exclaimed, and she flew home.

A few days later, Firenze received
a package...

DEAR FIRENZE,
I MADE THIS SKIRT
JUST FOR YOU. I HOPE
YOU WILL WEAR IT
TO MY ART SHOW
TOMORROW. YOUR
LIGHT IS A GIFT.
LET IT SHINE!!
LOVE,
KIRIE

Firenze felt nervous as she arrived at the art show the next day. But as her light glimmered through her skirt, she saw the faces of her friends.

While Firenze twirled on the stage, she realized how powerful her light was. It was creating magical art, joy for her friends, and happiness in her heart.

Suddenly, Firenze felt very grateful she was a firefly.

Firenze grew to love her light, even when it was difficult.
She always remembered the night she let her light shine for everyone to see.